Ghostwing

Au best wishes,
Kenn Steven

MOGZILLA

CABOODLE

First published by Mogboodle in 2013.
Paperback edition.

ISBN: 978-1-906132-89-7

Text copyright Kenneth Steven.
Cover by Andrew Minchen.
Cover ©Mogzilla 2012.

www.mogzilla.co.uk/ghostwing

T he boy liked looking out of the window, especially now that it was autumn. He crouched on the old chest that once had belonged to his mother and now was his, and he looked out over the fields.

Everyone else hated this time of year, the last bit of autumn. They moaned about it and wished it would be over. He looked at it now. The fields were filled with ditches of water that reflected the grey sky. The far trees were almost invisible because they were misty; it was as though they were not there at all. Up above them the low hills were grey too; the boy could only just make them out. It was true that everything was grey, but it was not true that it was boring and miserable. This was the most magical bit of the whole year, when anything might happen. At night the great winds came and shook the skies and woods; it felt as if the house might take off. Sometimes the boy woke in the night and did not want to go back to sleep; it felt as if he was in a great ship. His cabin rocked from side to side in the storm…

'Can you get in some coal?'

He was pulled from his thoughts by his father's voice. He turned round but his father had gone already so he didn't answer. He didn't want to go but he knew he'd better all the same. He slipped downstairs and put on his boots in the porch, picked up the bucket. Outside he heard something as his feet crunched the gravel to go round the side of the house. A single noise, then others. Somehow he remembered and looked up, but he could see nothing. It was the geese! The geese had come back from Iceland!

All that night he heard them. They were lost in the

misty skies and they were circling the house. Their cries sounded like rusty wheels and they drifted in and out of his dreams. The night wasn't stormy, that was why the mist hung as it did. He thought about their journey, that whole journey across the seas from Iceland. And they came back to the very same field as always, year after year.

*

The boy's mother had not come back. She was ill for two years with a disease called cancer. The doctors kept saying that she would get better but she never did. She had died in November.

He had come back from the hospital that night with his father. The car had been warm. It had rained for a whole week and now there were deep pools that almost flooded the road completely. It was a back road, a road that could take you to the city hospital all the same. But almost no cars used it nowadays; they went by the motorway in almost half the time. The boy didn't remember seeing one other car the whole way home.

He thought that somehow the skies and the trees had cried for his mother; they had all cried and these were their tears. This was what they had given in their sadness. The car was warm but he wished instead he could have got out all the same and walked into the woods. He believed somehow that there he would meet his mother. She would come walking towards him and everything would be all right, everything would be as it used to be. But they drove on, mile after mile through the strange darkness and the floods, and he felt enclosed in a cocoon. It felt as though he was wrapped in a kind of wool and he didn't even know if he could move his hands or his feet. And afterwards he wasn't sure if he and his dad had spoken or not. He only remembered the darkness and the floods and the warm car, and it was as if he was not really there at all.

His mother had said his name. She had recognized him and whispered Douglas, and he had reached out and held her. What he didn't understand was that she looked no different. Her face was the same as always, and her voice. How could she be dying then? That was why he had believed the doctors when they said she would get better; he had believed it was true because she never looked ill! And perhaps that was why he felt sure she was still there, out in the woods – that one day he would find her.

*

He woke up early in the morning and knew he had to go outside. The room was cold, but that didn't matter. He slipped out of bed and got dressed, softly opened the door and crept downstairs. He did not want his father to know he was going out. It was Saturday. Everything about school could be packed away in his mind and forgotten. He put on his boots and clicked the back door shut behind him. There wasn't a single sound in the world.

He went down to the bottom of the long garden, past all the old apple trees, to the little stile that crossed the fence into the field. He liked moving quietly, feeling he could pad so softly he disturbed nothing at all. There were some of the geese. They were called greylag. They nestled in the long grass, some still asleep, others looking with their golden yellow eyes. It was hard to see them since the field and the sky and the hills were grey too. He stood and just watched them. Then he took a path down the field. He felt the rain on his face, not really rain but more a mist of grey drops. It was soft and gentle; the year was still not cold. And then at last he heard something, a strange noise from the long grass – a squabbling sound, like nothing he had heard before. He went towards it quickly and saw something moving, rolling about in the long grass.

It was trying to get away from him but he was quicker than it was. He ran over and crouched down by a deep clump of grass and it was a goose, a toppled-over goose. He said soft words so it wouldn't be afraid but it kept squabbling and trying to get away. It was injured; there was something wrong with one of its wings.

Perhaps it had fallen; he wasn't sure. He had to help it; that was the only thing he knew for sure. Without thinking, the boy lifted the bird into his jacket and began carrying it back the way he had come. It was much bigger and heavier than he had imagined it would be and it snapped

6

at his hands as often as it could. He bit his lip because it hurt a lot but he didn't stop. He had to keep going.

*

The old shed hadn't been used for years. It was stuffed with paint pots and cupboard doors and broken handles. It was the place where Douglas' father put things he was going to mend and never did. One of the window panes was cracked – and had never been mended.

It wasn't easy getting the door open with a goose in your arms, a goose that kept stabbing at your hands all the time. Douglas staggered in, kicking a paint pot with his foot. In front of him was an old table covered with tubes of glue and cloths and broken dishes. Douglas swept all that away and put the goose down, but it was still just lying on a fold of his jacket. At least now he could rescue his hands; they were red and raw and sore.

He looked all round the shed. It still wasn't properly light and it was difficult to see things. Then, under a pile of broken baskets, he recognized the dog basket that once had belonged to his father when he was a boy. He had had a spaniel called Teddy.

Douglas slid the goose from the fold of his jacket onto the table and immediately it fell onto one side with its injured wing. The boy stumbled forwards and reached out to move the broken baskets. Something crunched under his left foot. He stretched a little further and caught hold of the edge of Teddy's basket. There was still a rough woollen rug inside. There was nothing for it but to lift the goose back in. He bit his lip. Another finger got nipped by that fierce beak but finally the goose was in. Now it was lying on one side, its good side. At least here it would be safe and warm. He'd leave the shed door ajar; there was nothing precious in there. Everything was broken, even the goose. He would come back with food, once he'd had time to work out what food would be best.

And then he heard the back door opening up at the house.

'Douglas! That's breakfast in five minutes!'

*

Later that day he managed to look at the Internet to find out what greylag geese ate. But it was frustrating. The Internet wanted to tell him where greylag geese came from, where they flew to, how far they could fly at one stretch, and why they were called greylag – but he couldn't find a single thing on what they ate.

But when he was looking out of his window, sitting on his mum's old chest, watching the grey fields under the grey skies, he suddenly realised something. The geese had nothing special to eat there. These were just fields that had had crops earlier in the year; they were full of stubble. So before it got dark he managed to sneak back over the stile and run down towards the stream that snaked through the field. He picked a handful of stubble with his sore hands. Then he ran back up to the shed and went inside. He took one of the broken baskets and filled it with bits of stubble for the goose. Then he found a plastic bowl and filled it with water. He put both down in Teddy's old basket and got just one peck from the goose. That was something else to find – a pair of really tough gloves.

The goose lay down on its side again and he didn't know what more to do. Maybe it would eat something once he had gone. He so much hoped it would survive, that it wouldn't die. In the shadows the boy saw the markings on its wings, how beautiful they were. And they weren't just grey, there was white there too. It was like people thinking autumn was only grey. Suddenly he wished he could have told his mum. He would have brought her out to show her what he had done; he would tell her about his sore hands but say that it didn't matter. Together they'd stand here and watch the goose.

But she wasn't here. It was getting dark and he had to go or his dad would get worried. He hoped so much that the goose wouldn't die.

'Good night, goose,' he whispered, and didn't know what else to say. Then he pulled the door to and chased up the garden to the house.

*

On Monday afternoon Douglas came home from school,

threw his bag in a corner of his room, and charged downstairs to make some toast. He was wondering how his goose was, looking forward to going to find out. His father came in with a cup of tea and sat down on the sofa.

'Douglas, d'you know where my new gloves are? The ones I got from your Aunt Helen? I can't find them anywhere.'

Douglas shook his head. He felt a bit of redness in his cheeks.

'And d'you happen to know what's become of that bowl from the bathroom cupboard? It's one I like to use for shaving.'

Douglas' face felt like a sunset now, but he didn't say anything.

'And you wouldn't by any chance have seen a little rug that's usually in the box by the front door? It's strange, it's completely vanished.'

Douglas didn't shake his head any more. His face felt as if it was on fire. He couldn't look away from his dad but he wanted to. He had felt so excited coming home. Now it felt as though the floor had fallen in.

'I happened to be down at the shed after lunch, Douglas – I was looking for something else completely. I found all those things, and the goose.'

It would have been impossible for Douglas' face to go any redder.

'You should have asked me, Douglas.' His dad didn't shout; instead his voice was quiet, and somehow that was even worse. 'You should have asked me before you just took those things. Imagine I went to your room and took things without asking. How would you feel?'

Douglas blinked. He had never thought of it like that.

'I didn't know what to tell you about the goose,' he said softly.

His dad nodded. He shrugged his shoulders and nodded again. Then neither of them said anything for a bit and Douglas just heard his heart, thudding under his jumper. Everything was so strange. He thought of things to say and then he didn't. It was like rubbing things out in school, writing a sentence and then rubbing it all out again.

Nothing he thought of seemed right or good enough.

'I'm sorry,' he whispered at last, looking up at his dad.

*

It was almost nine o'clock and time for Douglas to go to bed. He was upstairs, looking for this and that, when his dad came in.

'Put on your jacket and come out with me a minute,' he said. Douglas padded downstairs and found his shoes and jacket. His dad was waiting, holding the back door open. Where were they going?

Outside he saw the garage light was on and the car was parked in the drive. Were they really going somewhere? But his dad went into the garage. At the back was a shelf about the height of Douglas' shoulder. It had been a place for dumping old cases and boxes. Now it was clear.

'I thought this would be a better place for your goose. It's warmer here for one thing. And safer. There are so many broken things in that shed. The car can be in the drive; it'll be all right. So what d'you think? I'll help you up with the basket if you think it's a good idea.'

Douglas looked round. It was much warmer, and somehow nicer too. And it was easier to get to. He nodded; he looked at his dad and nodded. Together they went down the garden, past the shadows of the apple trees. In the end it was easier for his dad to carry the basket with the goose; Douglas followed behind with all the other things. His dad slid the box down onto the shelf at the back of the garage. The goose staggered over onto its good side again. Everything was very mucky in the basket.

'I'm afraid geese aren't all that clean,' said Douglas' dad. The boy could somehow hear him smiling even though he couldn't see him.

'You do know the goose might not make it?' he said softly, and now he turned round to Douglas. 'But we'll do our best all the same.'

And Douglas thought of his mum and suddenly couldn't say anything.

'It's funny seeing that old basket. It makes me think of Teddy, my dog, the first pet that was ever mine. Have you thought of a name for the goose, by the way?'

'I'm not sure, I'm still thinking. I want to find the right thing.'

His dad nodded. 'All right, one thing's for certain – we have to clean that basket. I'll lift the goose and get pecked

12

if you slide the paper underneath.'

*

That Tuesday morning Douglas' father went out to have a look at the goose. He changed the newspaper that lay underneath the bird and he got pecked again. The goose was still lying on its side. He thought for a while. After a few minutes he went back inside and phoned someone and asked if they would come round. In about half an hour a man carrying a bag came to the back door, and Douglas' father led the way round, and the two of them talked as they went.

The vet didn't say anything for a time. He leant over the basket that once had belonged to Teddy; he turned the goose over, gently.

'The wing's not broken, but it's obviously damaged. The bird's strong all right, it's not suffering. I can't say for sure what'll happen, John, but there's no harm in trying. It's a boy, by the way! And if the goose already means a lot to your son...'

Douglas knew nothing about this. While the vet was out in the garage, he was at school, busy working out maths problems – the thing he hated most. Outside the wind played and chased; the last leaves danced from the trees.

But after the vet left the house, Douglas had art. They were given charcoal and paper and told they could draw whatever they wanted. The teacher told the class he wanted them to be inspired by nature. Douglas drew a skein of geese. He had watched the skeins so often, coming in over the fields, one goose leading at the head of the v-shaped group. He had watched their heads and wings and feet; he had learned exactly what they looked like. As he drew he thought about his goose and wondered if it had been a leader.

This was when he felt happiest. He could forget about everything else, even missing his mum, when he drew. He didn't even find it difficult. It was as if the picture was there already; he could see it waiting to be found. The teacher came and watched him but he didn't say anything and Douglas didn't even know he was there, he was so far away in his mind. He'd just finished the picture when the bell rang out at last.

*

'Shall we go and remember your mum this afternoon?'

It was still half-dark in Douglas' bedroom, early on a Sunday afternoon. The boy had been asleep; he sat up now and rested on one arm.

'Could I take Ghostwing with me?' he asked, his voice still sleepy.

His dad's voice smiled. 'So that's the name for your goose. Yes, of course you can – you can hold the basket on your knee.'

They drove by the back roads. They always drove by

back roads. There was a chance they might see a rare bird or animal, and that day they both saw a bird with bright blue on its wings flying across the road.

'That was a jay!' Douglas' dad said, slowing down. 'We would never have seen that if we had come on the motorway.'

There was no-one else at the graveyard. It was gusty; the wind seemed to come from nowhere, as strong as horses. It was hard to walk straight. Douglas came up the path, carefully carrying the basket with Ghostwing.

'Why don't you sit for a bit on your own?' his dad suggested. 'I'll not be far away if you want me. I'll be back in a few minutes.'

Douglas nodded. He set the basket down and crouched beside the gravestone. His mum's name was there – Anne – but what he often wished was that it just said mum. Now his dad couldn't hear him; no-one could hear him. He began whispering to her all about how the goose had come, how he had gone out into the field and found him. He talked to his mum about his hands; he held them out and said he didn't mind they were sore as long as Ghostwing got better (that was the name he had given the goose, he told her). He would do everything he could to try to make the goose better and he would pray as well. He had drawn a skein of geese in class the other day…

And just at that moment he heard something. He looked up, startled, and saw that his dad was coming back towards him. But it wasn't that; it was something else he had heard…

He looked up into the sky and saw a whole skein of geese passing right overhead.

*

When they got back to the house they found there was a power cut. The wind must have blown down a power line somewhere, and now the whole village lay in shadow. Douglas couldn't help feeling excited; it was somehow like the old days, like a long time ago.

'Put the goose – Ghostwing – back in the garage, and bring in another bucket of coal. We'll put the fire on in the sitting room. How about that?'

When he came in he could hear the fire cracking and spitting. His dad had brought out an old kettle and there was a tray with shortbread.

'I forgot we couldn't make any tea,' he said. 'We'll boil the kettle over the fire, be like real gypsies!'

Later, once the fire was burning merrily and the room was warm, like a dragon's lair, Douglas' dad suddenly thought of something else. The two of them went upstairs with a torch, into Douglas' room, and over to the old chest by the window that had once belonged to the boy's mother. Douglas hadn't really ever thought of what was inside, and now he could see there were folders and folders of old pictures. He knelt beside his dad.

'I couldn't bear to look at these before,' his dad said

softly. 'But your goose has made me remember something, something you have to know.'

He rummaged and rummaged until he found a box at the very bottom.

'This is the one,' he said. 'Come down with me and have a look.'

They sat in the firelight and Douglas saw pictures of a young girl, not much older than he was now. Could that really be his mum? And there beside her was a goose – a greylag goose just like his.

'Your mum rescued this goose,' his dad told him. 'She loved geese just as much as you do, and she rescued this bird when it was shot and hurt. I don't think it ever flew again, but it stayed her pet until it died.'

His dad didn't look at him when he spoke and his voice was strange, as if saying some of the words was difficult. Douglas touched his dad's hand, just and no more. All of this seemed so strange.

'D'you know if the goose had a name?' he asked shyly.

'Yes,' said his dad, still not looking at him. 'It was called Littlewing.'

*

Even though his dad knew about the goose now, he still liked to go out on his own to see Ghostwing, especially early in the morning. Now it was December, and when he got out of bed just after half past seven, it was still completely dark. The room was cold and he shivered until he was dressed, then crept downstairs and clicked open the back door. Now it was getting colder. It was as if someone had very carefully sprinkled sugar on the tops of the faraway hills. Winter was coming closer.

He experimented with different green things for his goose. He found that Ghostwing liked Brussels' sprouts better than anything else (which Douglas couldn't understand at all – it was the one vegetable he would never, ever eat again – once had been more than enough.) His dad gave him pieces of leek to feed the goose (the pieces left over after he had peeled them.) They were long and stringy and the goose ate them gobble by gobble. But potato peelings were no good at all; Ghostwing nosed about with them a bit and then ignored them.

Douglas always fed the goose now with gloves on. Once he had forgotten and he had suffered a sore forefinger for the rest of that day. In the morning he liked to talk to the goose as he ate. It didn't matter what he talked about: school or friends or what was going to happen that day. He told the goose about the bullies, about what he would like to do to them if he had the chance. He talked about his mum too, about how much he missed her and wished she was still there. Then his dad would suddenly be at the back door calling him for breakfast. He'd tell the goose he had to go, switch off the light in the garage and charge up over the gravel drive.

His dad had put one of the pictures of his mum on

the living room mantelpiece, one of the ones with her and the goose. The colours were fading from the picture, from the edges, but it was still his mum. He liked to pick it up and look at it, look at everything in it, when his dad wasn't there. Somehow it felt as though his mum was still there, that she hadn't gone. It made him feel warm and good inside.

*

One night Douglas had a particularly vivid dream. He was struggling through a deep forest and at last he broke out into a clearing. It wasn't dark but it felt like dusk, just before nightfall. And suddenly there in front of him was his mum; she had crashed through into the clearing from another side. Her face was just the same as always but there was something different about her all the same. Douglas began talking to her, telling her all about the goose. And he told her why he had called his goose Ghostwing, that it was because everyone thought the autumn was grey and greylag geese were too, but that really they were silver and magical and ghostly. And she nodded and smiled and half-turned round so he couldn't see her face any longer, and in the last second he saw that she had wings, and she took off and flew out of the clearing and was gone.

He woke up, shivering and wide awake, thinking about all of it. He had wanted to say to her that they had almost chosen the same names for their geese, but she had gone before he had time. Now he remembered waking up in the morning a year ago knowing she was no longer there, that she had not got better at all. He had gone up to the wood above the house and somehow he had really believed he would find her. He would turn a corner and she would be there.

But the only thing that was there was the silvery, ghostly mist in the trees. Everything was still and silver, it was another world. And then when he broke out of the trees he heard the greylag geese moving about the field and muttering to themselves. It really sounded as if they were talking.

That morning he had an idea. He put on the bedside light, got up, and padded over to the old chest that had belonged to his mother, the one that had all the photographs. Carefully he brought out all the books of pictures. But there at the bottom was something else, a red book that was smaller and thicker. He lifted it, put everything else back, and closed the lid of the old chest. He padded back over to bed with the book in his hand. He opened it. It was a diary:

My father said that Littlewing won't fly again. I know that may be true but I don't want to believe it. That means he will never fly back to Iceland for the summer with all the other geese. Why do we have to shoot things? Why do we think it is always up to us to decide how many wild things there should be? I am still going to try to teach Littlewing to fly again. I have to keep believing it's possible. I won't say anything to anyone else but they can't

20

stop me hoping and believing.

*

Opposite, a single feather had been fastened to the paper. Douglas touched it softly with one finger. One of Littlewing's feathers. It was silver, it wasn't grey. He thought of what his mum had written and he wondered what had happened, if she had been right or not. He wondered if Littlewing had flown again after all. Then he remembered the year before, when she had been so very ill, when he had tried to believe with all his heart that she would get better. He had been so sure she would. But she hadn't. So it wasn't enough to wish or believe, not always.

Suddenly he realised he wished exactly the same for his goose. He wished that it would get better and fly again. But what if it didn't happen? What if it wasn't enough and his goose died after all? He felt terrified by the thought and he shut the red book, switched off the bedside light and hid in the darkness. But he couldn't escape the fear that whispered in his head. You could believe and hope as hard as possible, but it didn't mean something would happen all the same.

All at once he noticed the stillness. It was completely still. He sat up again and held his breath. It was getting light outside; it wasn't all that early. He thought, then he got up again and went over without a sound to his bedroom window. He pulled back a corner of the curtain and it was like opening an advent calendar window. The skies were dark and grey – no, they were silver. And falling from them, silver and huge and ghostly, were great flakes of snow.

*

He talked to the goose. He talked to the goose in exactly the way he had talked to his mother beside her grave. He talked to Ghostwing about school, about the boys who made fun of him in the gym class and about the teacher who shouted because he was no good at football. But he told Ghostwing about the art class, about how much enjoyed drawing and how particularly he liked drawing geese. Not just geese, but the fields and hills and everything else too. That was what he really wanted to do; he was going to be an artist. Then he stopped and thought about that. Was it going to be enough just to wish for that? He realised it wasn't. It would take hard work too. He looked down at the goose scrabbling about for the last Brussels sprout leaves in the box. This had to be about hard work too, if he really wanted Ghostwing to get better and fly again. That was at least part of it.

Suddenly he realised someone was there. He just knew it. He saw the shadow of his dad at the open door of the garage, a lantern in his hand. How much had he heard of what he'd said?

'There's another power cut,' his dad said, coming in, 'and the forecast is for more snow. So if you're lucky, a day off school tomorrow.' He put his hand on Douglas' shoulder and the two of them turned round.

'It's a bit like Bethlehem,' he said softly. 'I know there wasn't snow in Bethlehem, but it's a bit like the way I imagine it.' He stopped a minute. 'We'll try and have a nice Christmas, Douglas, even though your mum isn't here.' He turned to him. 'What d'you want as a present? What d'you want more than anything else?'

His dad looked at him in the shadows of the garage and all at once a wave broke over Douglas. He couldn't see any more for crying and he cried as if his heart would break. And his father set down the lantern on the garage floor and he hugged his son as hard as he could. He held him tight as the waves broke over him again and again. He cried for the one present he wanted so desperately and the one present he knew he could never have.

*

'Holly. We're going for holly.'

His dad had come to school to pick him up because there wasn't much time now before it got dark. He saw all the faces of the bullies: George Swinton, Alan Reardon, Tom McCarthy. And there was the worst of the girls – Abigail Edwards with her long red hair. She stuck out her tongue at him as the car drove away from school, up towards the wood.

'I have your boots and an old jersey in the back of the

car, his dad said. The road was almost clear of snow; what was left was slushy, like marzipan. But there were still lumps in the trees. Douglas just felt happy to be with his dad and to be away from school. This was good.

They tramped along the woodland path together and were as quiet as they could be. That was the best way to see things. All at once Douglas grabbed his dad's elbow and pointed away over to the right. There were three deer standing watching them. They stood stock still for a few seconds, and then they turned and vanished into the trees. And it was then Douglas remembered the dream he'd woken up to, the dream about his mum.

They found the holly trees and began clipping off little bits with berries. The holly was sharp, sometimes it hurt their fingers. It was waxy and had droplets of melted snow. The berries were bright and shiny.

'We'll pick a bit more than we need,' said Douglas' dad. 'We can give some to Mr Somerville, and to Mrs Ferguson across the road.'

Douglas nodded. Mr Somerville was afraid of falling in the snow and didn't come out much. Mrs Ferguson was very old and lonely.

The snow began again before they finished, but now what fell was quite different – it was like tiny ice needles. Douglas turned his face up to the sky and closed his eyes. The flakes fell like soft hair and brushed his cheeks and mouth. He suddenly thought that there should be lots of words for snow, not just one. There were so many different types of snowflake. He was still thinking about the best made-up word for this kind of snow when his dad came up behind him.

'Douglas,' he said. 'I have an idea.'

*

This was the idea. The pictures of Douglas' mum and her goose, Littlewing, had been taken about four miles away, at the top of a hill track. Her father had been a gamekeeper; he had to look after the estate lands, make sure fences were mended, watch out for poachers, keep an eye out for foxes. The family lived in a small cottage a thousand feet up on the hillside. It was called Applegarth. When Douglas' mum was growing up there everything had to be done by lamplight after it got dark because there was no electricity. But when she was fifteen her father had been given a different house much closer to the village. It was more modern, with electricity and a telephone. The old cottage on the hill was left empty. No-one ever went to live there again.

'So here's my idea,' Douglas' father said. They had had supper and were sitting by the fire. The holly they had gathered was in one big cupboard box, ready to be sorted out and shared with their neighbours.

'It would mean quite a lot of work. We'd take everything with us – and Ghostwing of course – and we'd go up to Applegarth for Christmas.'

Douglas' eyes lit up. He had seen the place where his

mum grew up from the outside, but he'd never actually been inside.

'I'll need to check with the estate,' his dad warned him. 'It will be cold Douglas, and you'll have to help with things. But it might be an adventure.'

There was no doubt in Douglas' mind. It was the most exciting thing he could imagine. He said yes about ten times, promised he would help, asked about all sorts of things his father didn't know the answer to, and then his dad reminded him he had a goose to look after.

'I'll phone the estate while you go and feed Ghostwing,' he said.

He was suddenly worried that the estate might say no. The place hadn't been lived in for years. Perhaps Applegarth wasn't even safe. He watched Douglas go out the back door singing, and all he could do was hope. He'd phone the new gamekeeper. Outside, Douglas had to tell Ghostwing the whole story. He forgot to whisper. When he came back inside he didn't say anything, he just looked at his dad.

'We can go,' his dad said softly. 'We can go there on Christmas Eve.'

*

It was the last day of school. There was a Christmas tree in the hall, lit up and covered with tinsel, a star glittering at the top. At eleven o'clock in the morning they all came in to sing carols. Douglas could see the snow through the windows. He could see right up to the hills above the village, and he thought of his mum. He thought of how she had come to this school too, and he wondered how she had got here every day. There were no big roads then, no mobile phones or modern cars.

'I hope you're all going to have a very special holiday,' said Mrs Anderson, their head teacher. 'I hope you'll have a happy time with your families, and that you'll remember this is a time to be especially kind, not just to the people we like – our friends and the people it's easy to be nice to – but to other people too. It's harder to be nice to the people who are different, who we may think are strange, but that's what we have to remember. That's the real message of Christmas for every one of us.'

The final shrill bell of term rang, and although all the teachers were calling out to them to walk quietly and keep in rows, nobody was listening. Children were shouting and screaming; they pushed their way out of the gym hall and Douglas felt an elbow in his ribs and someone kicking his heel. He turned round to see who it was and caught sight of Alan Reardon's face, laughing. He and Tom McCarthy were together, but he couldn't hear what they were saying. They were both trying to kick his feet and trip him up. They were both laughing.

He got out to the corridor and started fighting his way towards where he'd left his coat and bag. A teacher was somewhere close by, shouting instructions to the little ones and clapping her hands. Douglas reached his bag and then looked up, into the face of Abigail Edwards. She had been waiting. She had seen him coming. His hands were shaking.

'Hope you have a nice holiday, Douglas,' she shouted in his face. 'Oh, sorry, forgot your mum won't be there, will she!'

And she and Tom McCarthy and Alan Reardon shrieked with laughter, and disappeared together along the corridor, looking round at him as they went.

*

He didn't tell his dad about the red book, the diary. He wasn't even sure why, he just didn't. It was almost as if it was something his mum had given him, a present from her. He had woken up that first snowy morning after his dream about meeting her in the forest and he had suddenly known he had to look in the box. It was almost as if she had told him. He kept the book under his bed and he looked at it first thing in the morning and last thing at night. Littlewing and Ghostwing. He touched the goose feather on the last page of the book and he wondered and wondered what had happened. She had gone on believing her goose would fly again, even though she had been told there was no hope.

On Christmas Eve he felt so excited. After lunch they packed box after box – holly and lanterns and torches and food. He had to pack a rucksack with all his cosiest jumpers. The boxes piled up in the hall.

'Now if Santa could only deliver all of that straight to the cottage,' his dad said, clapping him on the shoulder and smiling.

'I think the reindeer have enough to do,' Douglas said.

Together the two of them packed the car. Douglas would carry Ghostwing on his lap. They were almost ready and it was just beginning to get dark.

'Matches!' his dad remembered, and rushed off to find them. That would have been a disaster: no fire, no dinner, no bedside lamps.

They drove up out of the village and the car felt weighed down. It was only five o'clock but everything was quiet, everyone was waiting now for Christmas. They drove past the last house and Douglas looked back into the valley. There wasn't a single other car. It was like it might have been a hundred years before. They turned off onto a single track road and the car whined and bumped its way along. Douglas got out and opened an old iron gate. There wasn't a single other house. They crossed a river whose banks were thick with snow. And then at last they were there. Douglas' dad switched off the engine and they got out. Douglas was carrying the goose. There wasn't a sound in the whole world.

*

It was good going to sleep by the light of the real fire. The logs were still burning, just and no more, in the grate. They glowed like dragon eyes.

By then it was midnight. It had taken a whole hour to get everything in and sorted. It was so much harder doing everything by candlelight. Douglas kept on forgetting and going to switch on a light. They sorted the kitchen first, then the little bedrooms at the top of the steep stairs.

'This was your mum's room,' his dad said quietly. 'You can have it, Douglas. You don't mind there isn't a curtain for the window?'

Douglas shook his head. He liked that. He lay on his bed later and could look right down over the valley. The moon would soon be full; it almost hurt to look at it, it was so bright. The snow glinted and there wasn't a breath of wind. There were no lorries to hear, no cars, no trains – nothing at all. He wanted to stay and keep looking, but he knew he should help his dad. And he had to look after his goose.

At the back of the house there was a small porch. He reckoned this would be the best place for Ghostwing, and using the glove he fed his goose a good meal. He was getting better at this now; it was very seldom he got his fingers nipped. Ghostwing still seemed to be weak on one side, but perhaps not as much as when Douglas first found him. That seemed a long time ago now – ages and ages.

He said goodnight to his goose and helped his dad with the fires. He gave a yawn and hoped his dad wouldn't notice. He was starting to get tired but he didn't want to sleep. This was too exciting. His dad heated up some milk over the fire in the living room and they sat hunched close to the flames, sipping piping hot cocoa.

Suddenly Douglas thought of something as they sat there not speaking.

'Are you glad we came here, dad?' he asked shyly.

His dad looked at him and nodded. 'I'd never have thought of it if it hadn't been for your goose and looking at the pictures in your mum's old chest. It's all thanks to your goose. Yes, I'm glad. I think your mum would be happy too. Perhaps she knows.'

*

Even though Douglas hadn't wanted to sleep right away, he had. He had cuddled into the blankets on the bed, looking at the red glow of the fire, and a moment later he was asleep. Across the hall in the other small room his dad fell fast asleep too. But about three in the morning he lay half-awake, aware of strange shadows in the room. He was lying on his back, the window ahead of him. There was no curtain on his window either. At first he was too far away in the world of his dreams to wonder what the shadows were, but at last he sat up. What was that light in the sky?

He struggled up. The room was freezing cold now the fire had gone out. He crouched beside the window, shivering. For a few minutes he watched the skies amazed, and then he knew he had to waken Douglas.

'You have to come and see this!' he whispered.

Douglas sat up, but he was still far away. At first he had no idea where he was. He felt woolly and strange, then he felt the cold. He whimpered his way into his clothes and moodily followed his dad downstairs. He had been so cosy. So why were they now going out in the middle of the night? He staggered outside into the snow that crunched with frost. His dad stood behind him and put his arms over his shoulders, bent his head to whisper close to his ear.

'Look up above the trees – no, further to this side. Right up, there – follow my finger. That's the north. D'you see the light? Coming and going, rising and falling? There, there was another! A green-blue colour – very, very faint. Now I know you think I was miserable waking you and it's the worst thing in the world, but I wanted you to see the Northern Lights. Look – that one was dark red!

Douglas stopped grumbling and looked. He could see them; shadows rising up like ghosts. They were beautiful and strange, like nothing else he'd ever seen.

They watched for half an hour until it got too cold, then they went back up into the darkness of the house. Douglas buried himself in the blankets. And very quietly, his dad left something that crinkled at the bottom of the bed.

*

Usually when he woke up, Douglas' first thought was his goose. But that Christmas morning his first thought was

32

the crinkling at the bottom of his bed. His second thought was just how cold it was in the room, but his first thought was definitely the crinkling. He had to deal with the second thought before the first, so he got up and tried to scrabble about to find a jumper. He kept on wanting to switch on a bedside light that wasn't there. It was still dark outside so the room was strange and shadowy. After a rather useless few minutes of rummaging without seeing anything clearly, he lit the candle his dad had given him. He took great care when striking the match, and though the candle wasn't the same as a light bulb, it did help. He cosied up in bed again, a thick woollen jumper over his thin pyjama top. Now he could work out what the crinkling had been.

He thought he knew what it might be – a stocking with all sorts of little presents. The year before there hadn't been one; it was somehow still too soon after his mum's death. His dad had given him a small present – he hadn't forgotten him – but neither of them had felt Christmas could be the same. There had been no snow, just rain and gales, so it hadn't even felt like winter in the end.

All of a sudden Douglas remembered going out in the middle of the night to see the Northern Lights. It felt like a dream now, but it had happened. His dad must have put the stocking there after they came in; it hadn't been there when he first went to bed. He thought about that as he sat with the stocking in front of him. He wanted to find a way of thanking his dad and he didn't know how.

At the top of the stocking was a little book of puzzles. Next there was a bag that was difficult to get out. What on earth was inside? At last he got it out – a bag of Brussels' sprouts. That had to be for Ghostwing, not him! He smiled. Below that was what felt like another book. He brought it out carefully, bit by bit, and gasped when it appeared. It was a beautiful sketch book, and below it a little box of charcoal. It was for his drawing. And finally, in the toe of the stocking, was a fat and juicy tangerine.

*

Douglas first thought of waking his dad right away to thank him. He went across the passage and opened the door of the other bedroom. He was about to open his mouth when he realised his dad was fast asleep. He didn't have to wake him now. He tiptoed out again and closed the door without a sound.

He went back to his own room, the room that once had been his mum's, and he saw all the gifts from the stocking strewn over the makeshift bed. He looked again at the really big present there, the drawing book and the box of charcoal. He saw the bag of sprouts too. A thought was taking shape in his mind.

He took those three things and went downstairs in his stocking soles. What were really cold were his hands. He could see his own breath. He went through to the little porch at the back of the house, expecting to find his goose wide awake and waiting for breakfast. But instead Ghostwing was lying on one side, the good side, his beak tucked into his wing. He was fast asleep. It was still shadowy in the back porch but there were more windows so it was easier to see. Douglas' heart thudded behind the thick jumper. His idea was going to work after all.

There was an ancient wicker chair in the back porch. The boy sat down on it and got ready. His hands were so cold. He cupped them and breathed warmth into them. Then he began drawing. He wanted to capture Ghostwing like that before the goose woke up, and he knew he had to work quickly. His fingers were trembling. Time seemed to stand still, just as it did in the art class. This was the best feeling there could be. He captured the shadows under Ghostwing's beak, where it tucked into the feathers of the wing. He found Teddy's old basket the hardest bit; twice he got it wrong and had to start again. He had to make it as accurate as he could; his goose really had to look nestled there.

At last it was done and he kept looking at it; his heart beat hard now because he was excited, he had done it. It was starting to get light. Then he had another thought. Yes, it was right, he'd do it! He crept upstairs to his dad's room. He was just turning over, beginning to waken.

'Happy Christmas, dad,' he murmured, and he knelt down beside him to give him the drawing.

*

'All right, it's a beautiful day – you and I are going on an adventure!'

The living room fire was burning fiercely; Ghostwing had had half the bag of sprouts and they had eaten a special breakfast – shortbread and cocoa, and an orange each. Douglas couldn't see his breath any more.

'What are we doing then?' he asked, curious.

'Surprise.'

That was all his dad would say.

'It has to do with your present, I mean your main present. That's still hidden in the car. So go and get ready and I'll see you out there in ten. Wrap up really warm.'

Douglas changed the paper under his goose and gave Ghostwing one more sprout. Then he put on all the warmest clothes he could find, even a bright red woollen hat his Auntie Elsie had given him.

'You look a bit like a holly berry,' his dad said when he got into the car.

But it didn't matter. There was no Alan Reardon or Abigail Edwards to see him now. He suddenly saw that this wasn't the top of the track. It went on, through the birch trees, snaking up the hill. The car didn't like the track very much; it skidded in the muddy snow and Douglas' dad drove very slowly and carefully. Douglas had to keep wiping the windscreen because it got so misted. Then, all of a sudden, a bright red sun burst over the top of the faraway hills and everything in its path was made rosy. Douglas' dad had to shield his eyes it was so strong. They came to a river and he slowed the car.

'I think this is as far as we should go,' he said. 'We can walk the rest of the way. Come on, I'm dying to show you your present!'

They got out and the only sound was the chatter of the water over the stones. There were little patches of ice among the rocks.

Out of the boot came something big. It wasn't a very neat parcel but that didn't matter. Douglas bent down to unwrap it with his gloved hands, but that wasn't going to work. With his bare hands he ripped away the paper. It was a sledge, a wooden sledge. Douglas gasped.

'This belonged to your grandfather,' his dad said. 'I've mended it, made sure it works, and now it's yours.'

By the time they got to the top of the hill and turned round, the car looked as if it was a toy. They couldn't see Applegarth at all, but a thin trail of smoke rose into the sky from behind a steep hillside.

'Ready?' his dad asked, once they'd got their breath back. 'I'll get on at the front and you sit behind me. It might be a bit slow the first time.'

But it wasn't. The snow wasn't deep on the hill, and it was crisp after several nights of frost. The sledge picked up speed and Douglas clung on as tightly as he could. His dad said something he couldn't make out and all at once they rolled over into a heap, and the sledge ran on ahead of them. Douglas' dad couldn't stop laughing. He lay on his back and made a snow angel with his arms, sweeping them up and down. He was covered in snow from head to foot.

'I'm too old for this,' he said. 'I'll never get up again!'

Douglas gave him a hand and they went back up to the top of the hill. This time his dad promised to steer better.

They set off and Douglas felt the breeze in his face. They went over a first bump and let out a whoop of joy; now they were steering between pine trees and the red sun flickered through the branches onto their faces. Douglas felt so happy. This was Christmas Day and he was with his dad. He closed his eyes and didn't want this ever to end.

'One more,' he begged, when the sledge finally ran out of steam.

'If you peel the potatoes, put crosses in the sprouts, set the table and do all the dishes.' His dad looked at him with one eye closed which always meant he was only joking, but Douglas still said yes.

On that last run he thought how much he wished you could slow down time. He wished you could speed it up when things were bad, but now he wanted to slow it down, to make all this last as long as he possibly could. Then he thought of his mum. He thought how much he wished she could have watched them and somewhere inside hurt. He missed her so badly. His dad ruffled his hair and spoke to him with such gentleness.

'Come on. Let's go back and make it a special day, a day to remember.'

*

By four o'clock it was dark. It had been the strangest Christmas dinner either of them had ever had, because all of it had to be cooked or heated over open fires. In the end Douglas' dad had heated old pans over two different fires in the house. There was no table in the house, so they'd had to eat crouched on the floor in front of the living room fire. But the mantelpiece was still there and it had a whole line of candles. When they had finished eating Douglas asked if they should do the washing up.

'We'll do it in the morning,' his dad said. 'Easier in the light.'

Douglas wasn't sure if that was an excuse but he didn't argue.

'Can I bring Ghostwing through?' he asked, suddenly thinking of his goose. He knew Ghostwing had no idea it was Christmas, but somehow it didn't seem fair leaving him out. His dad nodded and Douglas carried him through.

'To think some people have goose for Christmas dinner!' his dad said, looking over at Ghostwing who was nosing for a piece of sprout in the basket. Then he looked round at his son and his voice was soft and suddenly more serious.

'Are you going to be able to say goodbye to your goose, Douglas – if he is able to fly in the end? Are you ready for that?'

'I want Ghostwing to be happy. I found him with an injured wing and I want to make him better. It's just the same as it was with mum and Littlewing. She wanted her goose to get better, that was the only thing that really mattered.' He didn't know what else to say and he kept watching Ghostwing.

His dad nodded. He rocked on his heels where he sat and nodded.

'In a way it must have been much harder for your mum. Her dad was a gamekeeper and he used to shoot geese – he shot lots of things. Your mum hated anything to be shot – she had a soft heart just like you. So maybe it was even harder for her to keep the goose to begin with.'

Douglas nodded. He thought of the red notebook and the goose feather.

'It was a hard life in those days,' his dad went on. 'There wasn't much money at all. People who lived on the land were tough with animals – not cruel, but tough. They had to survive. So keeping a pet goose would have been a very, very unusual thing. Especially here and for that family.'

*

Douglas thought about all that for a bit. He stared into the orange flames and he could still hear his goose nosing about in the basket. He thought about his grandfather, his mum's dad, because he'd never met him. He had died just before he was born. He could just remember his other grandpa, his dad's dad. He had been kind and full of games and laughter. It was that grandpa who had made the sledge.

'What was mum's dad like?' he asked in the end. His face felt as it was burning, the heat of the fire was so fierce.

He moved away a little.

His dad sighed and thought a long time, working out what to say.

'It's difficult to answer, Douglas. You know what it would be like if I asked you what Abigail Whatshername is really like. Because she's horrible to you it would be hard for you to be honest about her. It's not that your grandpa was horrible to me but he didn't like me for a long time. He made it very hard for me to see your mum in the beginning.'

'Why?' Douglas asked.

His dad had pins and needles on the hard wooden floor and he took a blanket, folded it and sat back down. Again he didn't answer at once but stared hard into the flames, thinking and thinking about all of it.

'I wasn't from the land. My dad, your other grandpa, the one you remember and who made that sledge, he worked in a bank. I had grown up in the village. I didn't know about buzzards and rabbits and ferrets; I had never set a trap or shot something. I think your grandpa, your mum's dad, thought real men had to be like that. I think he wanted your mum to meet someone who would do all of those things – maybe a shepherd or a farmer or even someone like him, a gamekeeper. So for a long time I wasn't even allowed to go to the house. Your mum and I had to meet in secret. And once your grandpa caught me!'

Douglas' dad started to laugh. His face shone in the firelight.

'What happened?' Douglas asked, shifting about on the floor. 'Please tell me, dad!'

'All right. I'll make some tea first and then I'll tell you.'

*

Once they'd had their tea, Douglas' dad went upstairs with a torch to find something. He came back with a packet in one hand.

'I brought some of mum's pictures up from the house,' he said. 'I wanted you to get a sense of what it was like when she lived here.'

He sat down beside Douglas and opened the packet carefully. There was his mum as a little girl. She had long hair and she was holding a cat in her arms. The cat looked almost as big as she was.

'That cat was called Bawdruns,' his dad told him. 'It was the first pet she was allowed to have. But he wouldn't have been just a pet. He'd have had to earn his keep by catching mice. And probably he wouldn't have been allowed to stay in the house. He would have had a place out in the shed and he would have got the odd saucer of milk.'

Douglas suddenly remembered. 'But you didn't tell me the story, something about grandpa catching you! Please, you promised!'

'Well, your granny and grandpa were supposed to be going to the big town one Saturday. Your mum got a message to me the day before that they'd be gone all day. So I turned up at the house and walked right in the front door – I didn't even knock. Your grandpa was so furious he got his gun out of the cupboard and chased me three times round the house! I was scared out of my wits but I don't think the gun was even loaded. He chased me right out of the garden and I didn't see your mum again for nearly a month. I missed her so badly.'

His dad stared into the fire and Douglas watched him for a moment. He knew his dad was sad; he was thinking about how much he missed her now too. Douglas hadn't really thought about that before. He had only thought how he missed his mum. That had been what mattered.

'And how did you get grandpa to like you in the end?'

Now his dad was smiling again. He had turned round with a broad grin on his face. He put a new big log on the fire.

'Are you ready for another story then?' he asked.

Douglas smiled. Of course he was ready.

*

'Your grandpa said that I had to catch a fish. He didn't say this to me; he said it to your mother because I still wasn't allowed in the house. But he told her I could come in on condition I came with a fish, a fish I'd caught myself.'

Douglas frowned, thinking. He had never seen his dad with a fishing rod and he couldn't imagine him fishing.

It was a very weird thought indeed. His dad knew exactly what he was thinking.

'Nobody in my family fished, Douglas! He was right – we were all townies! It wasn't my fault I couldn't fish – there had been nobody to teach me. But I would have done anything to see your mum, so I borrowed all sorts of books from the library and found out where I could get a fishing rod. Oh, and by the way, I had to catch the fish on my own – I wasn't allowed any help from your mum. So, I went up by myself to this lake in the hills where I had been told there were lots of fish. I was so nervous I tripped and fell, got soaked even before I'd started fishing! I remember it was a miserable day, cold and wet, and all I wanted to do was come home and have a bath. I could hardly move my fingers they were so frozen.'

'But did you get a fish in the end? Was it worth it?'

His dad smiled and shook his head. 'I caught a fish that was the size of your pinkie, Douglas. I think that fish felt sorry for me and decided it would jump onto the end of the line. So that was what I came back with.'

'And what did grandpa say?'

'He roared and roared with laughter. He had never laughed so much in all his life, that was what your granny said. He laughed until he cried. He said he was going to stuff that fish and put it in a tiny glass case, though in the end the cat got it. But it didn't matter. I think in a way he was proud of me for what I'd done. From then on I was allowed to come to the house and I was allowed to see your mum. And in the end I think he liked me. It took a long time, but I think that finally he accepted me.'

Douglas nodded. But suddenly he was thinking about something else, about two things – Littlewing and Ghostwing. And about his grandpa.

*

'What do you think he would have thought of me?' Douglas asked.

'I think he would have been proud of you,' his dad said. 'Look what you've done for your goose. Ghostwing isn't flying again, but he's still alive. Even I know that many things we rescue from the wild die. They often die quickly, for all sorts of reasons. Ghostwing is a whole lot stronger than when you first found him. There's still a long way to go, but you've worked hard to make sure you did the best you could. You've gone out early in the morning in the dark; you've gone out at night when it was snowing. I really think he'd be proud of you, Douglas, even if he didn't tell you he was. He never really gave compliments; he didn't know how to.'

Douglas felt strange. He looked at his dad and wasn't sure what to say.

'And I tell you something else he'd be proud of, and that's your drawing. He was good at doing little sketches of wildlife, but he never really had a chance to learn. He left school at fourteen – think about that! He wasn't much older than you. But you have a real gift and he would be very proud of that. If he were still alive he'd take you to see eagles and otters and all sorts of other things. And you have got talent, Douglas – real talent. That drawing you gave me is amazing. And most of all, your mum would be proud – that's for sure.'

There was something funny in his voice when he said that, and Douglas just nodded too. What a strange Christmas Day it had been. Like nothing he had ever believed it might be, but good, special.

'So, are we going back down to the village tomorrow?'

'Please can we stay one more night, dad?' he begged. 'I love it up here and we might never come back, this might be the only time.'

His dad nodded. 'We don't have all that much food but we can graze on leftovers. All right, we'll stay tomorrow night too. Come on, let's get a long good sleep. I'm still sore after all that sledging!'

But when they went upstairs Douglas sat by the window in the room that had been his mum's. He thought about so many things and he wished she was still there to ask all sorts of questions. He had learned so much he didn't know, but it was only a beginning. There was so much more.

*

Boxing Day was always a day when Douglas felt down, but this year it seemed worse than ever. Christmas Day was over, that was no different to other years, but everything now felt completely grey and miserable. The fires that had burned so merrily had turned to ash and every room in Applegarth was freezing. In the kitchen all the dishes lay piled in a heap, unwashed and stuck together. Outside it was drizzling. But more than anything and everything else that morning Douglas missed his mum. She felt all around them in that house and yet she wasn't there. It was like so often when he had believed all he needed to do was go up into the wood and she'd be there, coming to meet him. Now he felt he should be able to go upstairs and hear her voice, calling him. She was so nearly there and yet she wasn't there at all.

His dad still wasn't up and he let him sleep. He went and found his precious new drawing pad and box of charcoal, and he went back to sit in the wicker chair to do another drawing of Ghostwing. But his goose was wide awake, moving constantly about the old basket, never in the same position for more than a few seconds, and Douglas gave up in despair. His hands were red with cold anyway; it was hard to hold a bit of charcoal. He went back into the living room and he thought he'd give his dad a surprise by getting the fire lit again. It was a messy job and all he managed to do was get his hands and face filthy. He felt cold and miserable and he missed his mum so badly, and he cried there where he sat, crouching by the old hearth. And that was how his dad found him twenty minutes later when he came downstairs. He crouched down beside his son and reached out for his freezing cold hands.

'Forget the fire, I'll do that. You worry about that

goose of yours. I reckon he needs a bit of exercise and I want you to try to take him for a walk. By the time you get back I'll have had a thought about what we can do today.'

He gave Douglas a big hug and ruffled his hair. Douglas tried to smile. He put on a huge jumper and his boots to go outside. His dad went into the kitchen and came back with a saucer of torn up Brussels sprouts.

'That's for Ghostwing,' he said, 'but just one bit at a time.'

*

Douglas quickly got a hang of the plan. The way to lure Ghostwing a bit further was to crouch with a bit of sprout a few yards away. Ghostwing looked up, saw the open hand with the tempting piece of sprout, and reluctantly began to waddle over. His goose still wasn't steady on his feet and still seemed to lean to one side. But his dad was right that Ghostwing was stronger; there was no doubt about that.

All at once a picture flashed into Douglas' mind. He saw his mum crouching on these same stone steps at the back of the house, trying to get her goose to walk and become stronger. He felt so certain that that was how it had been, and he imagined his grandfather at the back door, watching. His grandpa had shot geese, and he thought just how hard it must have been for his mum to be allowed to keep an injured goose. His mum must have been very determined indeed.

And then he heard something. As he crouched in the wet snow, trying to lure his goose a little further, he heard a sound he recognised. He looked up into the sky and there was a skein of geese, calling as they flew. They were right above him, just as the geese had been the day they went to visit his mum's grave. It was as if they had known he was there. Only Ghostwing paid them no attention at all and Douglas couldn't help laughing. Sometimes his goose was like a grumpy old man. He held out his hand.

'Come on, Ghostwing! It's your favourite! Come on, you can do it!'

His goose lurched over one more time and gobbled up the bit of sprout. Then Ghostwing lay down on his good side and would go no further. Douglas crouched there and talked to him in a low voice, saying he had done well and that next time they would go further. Ghostwing tucked his beak in his beautiful wing feathers and gave a sigh. Douglas stopped talking and looked round in the direction of the back wall of the house. Something was glinting. He got up to look, intrigued.

There was a key lying on the stones, right in against the house wall. It was about the length of his pinkie; it was smaller than a shed key. He turned it over in his hands. Where on earth did it come from?

*

It was much harder to get Ghostwing back to the house than it had been to get him out of it. Nothing seemed to work and after a long time of waiting, Douglas gave up and carried his goose back. He got one bad nip. Ghostwing was certainly not a tame goose, that was for sure. He put him down gently in Teddy's old basket and left him the last three pieces of sprout on the saucer. He still had the key safe in his left hand.

'Look what I've found, dad!'

His dad wasn't sure where it came from. He thought it might be from one of the sheds at the back, or that it had just been dropped by someone. It might be that it had nothing at all to do with the house.

In the living room there was a roaring fire, and over it his dad had a sizzling pan of bacon. They had two rolls each and piping hot tea.

'Now, while you were out I had an idea for something we could do,' his dad said. 'Your mum once showed me a place where she used to go sliding, and I reckon the ice'll be strong enough. So why don't we do the dishes first and then wrap up and see what it's like? We'll need to walk there.'

The dishes didn't take as long as Douglas had feared. His dad washed and he dried. The house was feeling warmer now and outside there was a tiny bit of blue sky in all the grey. Maybe it would turn bright after all. They packed a lunch and made a flask of tea. They changed into their warmest clothes and Douglas left the little key beside his bed. It winked silver in the light, just as when he had seen it first, and he wondered again where it had come from. Maybe his dad was right; maybe it wasn't even from the house but had been lost by someone else. His dad called him and he forgot about everything else. The last thing he put on was the red woollen hat from his Auntie Elsie. They were ready to go.

He told his goose where they were going and Ghostwing didn't seem the least bit interested. He just looked at Douglas with one eye and then went back to sleep. He had plenty of food if he was hungry. Douglas closed the door and went out.

'I think I remember the way. It's up through the wood and over the hill. I remember a red gate. I think we follow the track the whole way.'

*

That was the best day's sliding Douglas had ever had. It was an old skating pond and the water in it was shallow. Now it had frozen solid. It hadn't been all that easy to find, though. His dad had been right about a red gate, but not right about following the track the whole way. After the red gate there was a little path that led through the woods. The pond was completely hidden; there were tall trees on every side. In the end Douglas could take a long run and then slide the whole length of the pond. Once he let out a whoop of delight and a whole flock of pigeons scattered from the trees. He kept sliding until he was out of breath and very warm. Then he sat down with his dad and lay on his back until he had his breath back. There was pure blue sky above him now.

'Listen,' his dad whispered suddenly.

He did listen, still on his back. There was a murmur of breeze in the trees and then there was complete stillness. There wasn't a sound in the world. Douglas suddenly thought that they hadn't seen another person since Christmas Eve. It was amazing when you thought of all the millions of people there were, and yet now it didn't seem as if there was another living soul around. Douglas sat up on his elbows and thought of something else.

'Did mum miss living up here, when they moved to the village?'

'I know she did, I remember her telling me. She said she cried for two whole weeks. She used to come back whenever she could, just to see Applegarth and to come to places like this. But in the end she had to start a new life. It was too sad coming to see an empty house.'

Douglas was imaging it, imagining what it must have been like.

'Can we come up here more often, dad? I mean to explore, to find places like this that mum knew? I like it, it feels right.'

His dad looked at him and he nodded, understanding. He almost smiled but not quite and he kept nodding.

'Of course we can. I think I feel the same, even though it can be hard at times. We'll come up and explore, as often as you want to.' He paused. 'Come on, let's have some lunch and then get back before it's dark.'

*

They went to bed early again that night. Maybe it was partly the dark outside; it made you think it was later than it really was. They had a piece of Christmas cake and cocoa in front of the orange embers of the fire, then Douglas made sure his goose was all right and they blew out their candles and went upstairs. They had made fires in the bedrooms too and Douglas put a new log onto his fire before he got ready for bed. He was determined to watch the flames when he was tucked up in bed; he wanted to remember this as long as he possibly could, and this was their last night. Tomorrow, life would be back to normal once more.

He managed a few minutes and then he almost drifted off. He shook himself awake but his eyelids were heavy and this time he fell asleep properly. He dreamed he was drawing in the art room at school. He was drawing a whole skein of geese on one great big sheet of paper and he knew that all the bullies were watching him. He felt his hand trembling as he drew but he knew he could do it all the same. They were laughing at him, calling him all the worst names they could think of, but he didn't turn round – he kept on drawing. And he knew in his heart the drawing was for his mother. It had to be a present for her.

Then he woke up, was wide awake in a second, and he wondered what it was that had woken him. He was lying on his back and the moon was shining in the window. The fire had gone out but the room had turned to silver in the moon's light. He looked at the wall beside him and he saw the light was shining on a keyhole. There was a cupboard in the wall, not quite as tall as he was.

A mad thought went through his mind – what if the key fitted, the key he had found that morning? For a second he couldn't face the cold; then he made up his mind. He had to know now; he wouldn't sleep again if not. He flung off the blankets and pulled on his jumper, shivering madly.

He picked up the key, held it, reached out to the lock. And it fitted. He turned it and the door opened. It was stiff and he had to pull it open.

And there on the other side lay a small red notebook.

*

Douglas lit the lamp by his bedside. His hands were still shaking. This felt like another dream, but he pinched himself and it wasn't. He kept his jumper on and got back in to his makeshift bed. Then he opened the book and read:

This spring I have been walking with Littlewing, a little every day. My dad still says the goose will never fly again, but I can't give up hope. I want Littlewing to be well. I want him to fly back to Iceland with the others. I have to hide away pieces of food for Littlewing; my mother
54

won't give me anything. She says it is a sin to give up food for a goose when there are starving children in the world. She is sometimes more strict than my father. I go out with Littlewing very early every morning, before it's properly light.

Then there was a new date on the handwritten entry, from early February.

In some ways my father is more interested in the goose than my mother. He still doesn't believe that Littlewing will ever fly again, but now and again he will come to watch the goose at the back door. It's not my father's fault that he shoots so many things; that's how he was taught to be when he was a boy. He learned then that there were too many geese and that their numbers have to be kept down. All the other gamekeepers say the same thing too, so he's never going to listen to someone like me. But I am almost sure he does see that my goose is intelligent all the same. Perhaps he has learned to look at them in a new way.

Douglas forced himself to stop reading too quickly. This was the next part of the story, the story that had ended in the red book he had found at the bottom of the old trunk at home. But why had the book been left here in the cupboard? It was almost as if his mother had known he would come here one day and find it. There were so many things that had happened since he found Ghostwing. Had his mother come back to the house after they moved to the village to leave the book and the key here? He might never know.

Littlewing has flown! Just a few yards, but he has flown all the same! My father said nothing when I told him, he just nodded. My father always says something, but now I really believe he was lost for words. It's as if he's in shock. He's very quiet and gentle, as if he can't quite believe what he has heard. My mother said nothing at all when I told her; she still believes Littlewing should never have been kept alive after he was injured. A goose that is shot is for eating, that's what she believes. There is nothing I could ever say to her that would change her mind.

Douglas turned the page, his eyes flickering over the words. He had to read on; he couldn't stop now.

This morning my father came out to see Littlewing. I crept downstairs as usual to see how my goose was, and there was my father. He tried to pretend it was an accident he was there, but I know it wasn't. Littlewing is very restless. The other geese are restless in the fields too; it's almost time for them to fly back to Iceland after the winter. When I walked with him today he was restless and looking in every direction. He didn't fly but he was trying to stretch his wings all the time. My father kept watching at the back door. Then he disappeared when he saw my mother.

Douglas was shivering; it was so cold in his mum's old room, but he had to know how the story ended. He would never sleep if he didn't find out! His eyes scanned the words as quickly as possible, but even in the lamplight it was hard to read the words, and his mum's handwriting wasn't always clear. One thing was absolutely certain, he was wide awake. He forced himself to get up again and put on a second jumper. He glanced out of the window and saw everything silver in the moonlight. It was so beautiful. He thought what it would have been like to grow up here instead of in the village. Then he thought of how hard his granny and grandpa had been on his mum. It wouldn't have been easy; in a way it was a whole different world up here. He suddenly imagined what it would have been like if he'd had to beg his dad to be allowed to keep Ghostwing. But now he had to know what happened to Littlewing, to his mum's goose.

This morning I went out a bit later. It was a clear day, with a little new snow on the hills. My father was there too, and this time he didn't pretend it was by accident. What happened was this. I gave Littlewing his food outside, and all at once we heard a skein of geese overhead. He lifted his head, tried his wings, ran as if to get up speed, and then rose into the air. For the first few seconds I wasn't sure if he would make it; I was afraid he might fall, and then he began to beat his wings. There was no doubt he had made it. I think I was crying and my father came and put his arm around my shoulder. I looked at him and he was nodding, nodding all the time. I was so happy, as happy as I've ever been in my life, and I wanted to say something and I couldn't. Littlewing had flown after all. He would go back to Iceland with the other geese. It had happened just as I had dared believe it might. But I couldn't have spoken. I was trying as hard as I could not to cry and the harder I tried the worse it was. It was the end of such a long struggle and it had happened after all.

Then my father did the last thing in the world I expected. He gave me a hug and he patted my hair. That made me cry all the more. "There, there, lass," he said in the end, and there was something funny about his voice, something I'd never heard before. And then he said something else I never thought he'd say in a hundred years. I almost fell over with shock when he said this, except it was more of a whisper than words out loud, almost as if he was afraid someone else might hear him:

"And I promise you that as long as I live I'll never shoot another goose."

When I turned round in the end there was mother standing in the doorway. She wasn't angry that we hadn't come in to breakfast. I think maybe she saw the moment Littlewing flew too. She never said a word about it, but I think that maybe she did. I smiled and went inside and perhaps I feel both of them look on me just a little differently now. Perhaps they have both seen I can do something for myself after all. It's not that I was right; it's more that I kept on believing.

When he went downstairs the following morning, Douglas almost believed Ghostwing would fly too. His head

58

had been full of his mother's story all night. But his goose didn't even want to come for a walk with him. Ghostwing seemed much more content with the warmth of the porch, even after Douglas had sat on the wicker chair and told him in a loud whisper the whole story of how Littlewing had flown again. Ghostwing was nosing about for a last bit of sprout. When he had found it he turned away from Douglas with a sigh and tucked his head under his wing. Douglas knew how hard it was to take a cat for a walk; now he knew it was even harder with a goose. He decided to go out on his own.

His dad listened to the story of the red book and didn't say a word. He let Douglas tell him the whole thing while he looked at the book himself and nodded now and again. When the story was done he looked up at Douglas.

'See how your mum kept on believing? She didn't give up hope. We'll take this back home with us and keep the two books together. I think she'd have wanted that. I want to read both of them the whole way through.'

'Why d'you think one of the books was in mum's old trunk and the other one up here at the house? Why weren't they in the same place?'

His dad shook his head and flicked through the pages of the book again. They were a little bit crinkled with age but everything could still be read.

'You remember I told you yesterday that your mum came back to the house? She came back because she missed all of it so much.'

Douglas nodded. He saw his mum in his mind's eye;

he imagined her up at the old pond and back here at the house, in her old room.

'There was no-one here after they left,' his dad went on. 'Maybe the house was even open. Maybe your mum actually wrote this book in her old room! I don't know, but perhaps she left it here in the end because it was a story that happened here. Somehow it belonged here.'

A noise made them both turn round. It was Ghostwing who had plodded in from the back porch. They both laughed.

'I think your goose wants a second breakfast! Then we'll need to get packed and go.'

When they came back the house was as cold as a snowball. There were one or two messages on the answering machine from people puzzled they weren't at home. Auntie Elsie who had given Douglas the red woollen hat wanted to know if her presents had arrived safely. She knitted all her gifts, so Douglas had a good idea what his would be.

He felt strange being back home. In one sense everything was so familiar and yet somehow it felt strange too. It was funny switching on electric lights again; he missed being able to light a candle or a lamp. But at least he could still help his dad make a roaring fire in the living room. They put on the Christmas tree lights and now it felt more like Christmas. It was still the holidays; there were days and days until he had to go back to school.

'Why don't we be good Santas?' his dad suddenly decided. 'We'll go round to the neighbours with a present, just like we usually do before Christmas. The holly's still in the box where we left it!'

That was a good afternoon. He had too much Christmas cake and his dad had too much mulled wine, but there were lots of stories about winter in the old days and snowstorms and people getting lost, and Douglas was glad they had gone out. He remembered what Mrs Anderson had said about the real meaning of Christmas, that it was about being nice and giving to other people, not just getting presents for yourself.

They went back home and his dad fell fast asleep in the armchair by the fire. Douglas tiptoed out and went upstairs to find his artist's pad and the box of charcoal. He did a sketch of his dad with his mouth open and he was pretty pleased with it. He left it on the mantelpiece so his dad would find it when he woke up. Then he remembered his goose; it was time he went out to feed Ghostwing.

He put on his boots and switched on the back door light. There was a light breeze in the garden, and he could hear it passing over the field. He'd give Ghostwing some sprouts; it was still Christmas after all. He switched on the garage light and quietly went up towards Teddy's old basket. He stopped dead in his tracks. Ghostwing wasn't there.

*

Douglas rushed inside and banged the door. His heart was hammering.

'Dad! It's Ghostwing! There's no sign of him! He's

gone!'

His dad was shaken out of sleep in a second and he grabbed his coat.

'Go and get the big torch, Douglas, the one we had up at your mum's house.'

They went out into the back garden and the old apple trees hissed in the wind. The torch beam flashed this way and that as Douglas' dad led the way down towards the old shed, the one where Douglas had hid Ghostwing when he first found him. The trees rattled with the wind and Douglas' hands were sore with the cold. It didn't matter, though – all that mattered was finding his goose. He followed the light of his father's torch, hoping and hoping he would suddenly spy the shape of Ghostwing, but there was nothing.

'You don't think someone would steal Ghostwing, dad?'

His dad smiled, and Douglas could hear the smile when he spoke.

'Anyone who tried to steal that goose of yours would get one heck of a bad nip! There are easier things to steal than a goose. Perhaps if he was laying golden eggs, but that hasn't happened yet. No, I think the answer will end up being a lot simpler than that.'

And so it was. After searching every square inch of the garden they decided to check the old shed. The door had been left open just enough for a goose to squeeze through, and that's exactly what Ghostwing had done. Douglas and his dad were so relieved that they both had to stand and laugh.

'Isn't that typical?' said his dad. 'You do all you can to get an animal – or in this case a bird – as cosy as you can, and it goes back to the very place you took it away from! Come on, we'll try the basket again!'

He carried a very grumpy Ghostwing back to the garage and got pecked a good number of times before he got there. But Ghostwing seemed to settle in the basket all the same. As they stood there watching, the rain began pattering on the garage roof and sounded like fingertips. They closed the door this time and went back up to the house, happy all was safe and well. Douglas felt his heart flooding with relief. He loved his goose. And suddenly he wondered how he ever really could face watching him fly away.

*

'I think it's a good sign,' said his dad when they were back by the fireside. Douglas looked at his dad. How on earth could Ghostwing disappearing be a good thing?

His dad put down his mug of tea. 'Think about it,' he said. 'Your goose was injured; there was something wrong with his wing. That was why he was all lopsided. The fact that he's able to get from one place to another, and quite fast, means he's much stronger. You started taking him for walks up at Applegarth, mum's old house, and I think it's had an effect!'

Douglas nodded. It was true; his goose was stronger. But he was thinking about something for the first real time. He was thinking what it would be like when Ghostwing flew away. That was what his mum had wanted for Littlewing, and that was what had happened in the end. She had cried, but more because no-one had believed her that her goose would fly again, and she had been right after all. Things were different here. His goose was getting stronger all the time and might well be able to fly, but was that really what he wanted? Of course he wanted Ghostwing to be well, but if his goose flew back with the skeins to Iceland, that would be the last Douglas ever saw of him. He knew for the first time just how much he would miss his goose. He had done so much for Ghostwing since he found him. He had hoped against hope he would survive and he had done. Would he be strong enough to say goodbye? What about afterwards?

He didn't say a word to his dad, but he went to bed that night with all of those thoughts circling in his head. He didn't sleep for a long time; he tossed and turned in the darkness. He knew what was right but he couldn't help being frightened of losing his goose. He didn't know what to do.

His dad had noticed Douglas had gone to bed worried, but he hadn't said anything. He wondered if it was coming back home from Applegarth. He wondered if Douglas was missing his mum. Or was it something else, something he couldn't work out? When he looked in on him at midnight his son was fast asleep, but the blankets were all twisted and muddled. He wondered what was worrying his boy. He had to work it out. It wasn't all that difficult to figure out what was wrong with Douglas. Over the next few days before the new year arrived, he didn't go out much with his goose. He made excuses about hail and rain, or he said he wasn't feeling so good, and he spent a lot of time on his own in his room. He said he was drawing, but when his dad said to him he should come down and draw in the warmth by the fire, Douglas muttered an excuse.

One night his dad went upstairs and sat at the bottom of his bed. He looked at Douglas in a certain way, when he wanted to have an honest answer and wouldn't go away without one. Douglas knew that look very well indeed.

'What is it?' his dad said. Just those three words, and the look.

Douglas sighed. He turned round in bed but he knew it was useless. He knew his dad would stay until five in the morning if he had to.

'It's Ghostwing,' he said, his voice very low and muffled by a blanket.

Now his dad came and sat beside him. His voice was different this time.

'I guessed it was Ghostwing, but what exactly?'

Douglas sighed again and couldn't look at his dad. He felt so confused.

'I want him to fly but I don't. If he flies then he won't come back.'

And then his eyes filled with tears and his dad hugged him a long time as he cried. His dad didn't say anything at all; he just held him. Then he went downstairs and made them both mugs of cocoa. He put on the bedside light and Douglas sat up against his pillow, his eyes red. Still his dad said nothing. Douglas kept waiting for him to speak.

'I thought you would be angry,' he said in the end. 'That it was bad to think like that.'

'What can I say?' his dad said. 'I understand completely. I bet I'd feel the same. You want two things and you can't have both. The only thing I'm sure of is that I bet your mum felt the same sometimes. I bet she did. It's hard to give something that you love back. In a way it was the same with your mum. I loved her and I had to let her go; I had to say goodbye, even though I never wanted to. I didn't want her to suffer, but I didn't want to say goodbye. So how could I be angry or think that what you're frightened of is bad? I understand completely. That's the truth.'

*

So his dad went with him when they walked Ghostwing in the field. Sometimes those walks were very frustrating indeed. Ghostwing would sit down in the grass and look at them both as if to say: 'You can try to make me go further, but you're not going to manage!'

And it didn't matter if they tried to lure Ghostwing with pieces of sprout, or cabbage or carrot – the goose just closed his eyes and ignored them.

'Come on, we'll go for a walk ourselves!' Douglas' dad would say to his son.

They walked down to the bottom of the stream in the field, their hands deep in their pockets because it was freezing, even though there wasn't any snow. Then, on New Year's Eve, the last night of the year, it snowed until the little shed at the bottom of the garden looked like an igloo. Douglas sat at the upstairs window, hoping it would go on and on so there would be no school at the end of the week. But by then the snowploughs had got to work and the blocked roads were unblocked, and Douglas sat in the school hall feeling as though he had swallowed a dark knot. The whole term stretched ahead of him. When he turned round he caught sight of the faces of George Swinton and Alan Reardon. Last of all he spied Abigail Edwards; she glared at him and stuck out her tongue. He remembered what she had said on that last day before the holidays and he thought how they were over now – all the days up at his mum's old house and the days at home. They had seemed to stretch for ever and now they were over.

Mrs Anderson got up and clapped her hands. Slowly a ripple passed through the classes until not a single sound could be heard.

'Welcome back, all of you, and I hope you've had a wonderful holiday. Now we're back at school and the hard work begins again today. Can I remind you of an art competition for all the primary schools in the county? Entries have to handed in by the end of the week and as we've lots of budding artists, I want to see plenty of entries! Have a good day in class and remember there'll be no outdoor playtime today because of the snow!'

Douglas got up, his head spinning. An art competition: would he have time to draw something new? His heart hammered in his chest as he went out into the corridor.

*

'I'll tell you what you're going to draw, you're going to draw that goose of yours,' and his dad pointed at Ghostwing as they stood together in the garage. 'And your drawing's going to be as good as the one you did for me!'

So after school that Monday afternoon, Douglas sat in an old chair in the garage a little way away from his goose. Ghostwing wasn't the least bit interested, had his beak tucked into his wing. He sighed occasionally. Douglas was sitting on a blanket and he had another blanket around his shoulders. He had his Auntie Elsie's red woollen hat on his head. His dad asked if he could take a picture of him, and Douglas said that if he did he wouldn't dry another dish for the next ten years. So his dad didn't risk it and instead he brought Douglas his sketchbook and box of charcoal.

For a bit, Douglas couldn't really begin. His hand was trembling; he felt nervous. He had to forget all about the competition, he realised – this was just another drawing. It was no different to being in the art room. He had to forget about everything else and find the goose that was hiding in the paper. Twice he began and twice he started again; he had to crumple up the bits of paper and put them under his chair so he didn't see them. It was going to be dark soon. He had to get it done.

And then it was as if the piece of charcoal began to move in his hand. He could start to see his goose on the page. The angle was different, but it was very like when they had been up at Applegarth, his mum's house, and he had sat on the old wicker chair to draw his goose in the back porch.

In half an hour he was finished. Now his hand was trembling again, but it was because he had done it – he had managed it after all. He took the blankets and he went inside. He just knew his dad was upstairs and he climbed slowly, looking at the drawing in his hand as he went. He knew there was nothing he could do to make it any better. He met his dad on the landing and he didn't say anything either, neither of them did. His dad was drying his hands. He looked at the drawing and he looked at his son. Douglas felt a glow of pride because he knew his dad was pleased. He had done it. He had done the drawing in time.

*

He loved autumn, he always had, and his mum had loved it too. They used to go for long walks together, before she fell ill and was in and out of hospital. They loved exploring the wood together, looking for conkers under the best of the chestnut trees, and watching for red deer and squirrels and owls. The wood was another world; it was somewhere the bullies could be forgotten. It was a land where homework did not exist; somehow there was no time there.

But the spring was different. The silver he loved so much had been washed away by the winter. Christmas and New Year were over; there wasn't a single sign of life in the fields. Everything was grey.

So once the drawing had been handed in and forgotten, his heart felt heavy. Every day he dreaded the taunting of Abigail Edwards and the others; there was nothing he could do to make them leave him in peace. It was as if Christmas had been a dream that now had faded; his dad was busy with work and there wasn't time for walks. He looked after his goose every morning and every evening, but at the back of his mind was always this fear that when spring came Ghostwing would fly once more and be gone for ever.

One morning, when Douglas was at school, his dad called his friend the vet and asked if he would look round. At lunch-time he came and the two men went down the gravel drive to the garage as they had before.

'This is a much stronger goose,' the vet said at last. He sounded surprised.

'Will he fly again?' Douglas' father asked quietly. 'Is it likely?'

'John, I can't tell you that – I don't know. But there's very little wrong with this goose now – that much I can tell you. Douglas has done well.'

His dad nodded. He had done well. But he was afraid

70

of his son having to lose his goose too. He had lost too much in his life, too much of what he loved. He didn't tell Douglas the vet had visited; there was no reason to tell him. The goose had brought so many special things, surely it couldn't all end now, not with nothing? It was raining outside and everything was grey – the skies, the hills, the fields. He had to keep hoping and not give up, but it was hard. He read the little red book Douglas had found in his mum's old room. He read it at night to find comfort, and because he hoped he might just find something else – another answer.

*

But the spring came, bit by bit. The streams rushed and chattered with melted snow, and the first weak yellow sunlight shone through the valley. The birds sang again, and even the high hills were clear of snow once more. The days were longer at last and the colours that seemed to have gone for ever crept back one by one. In school Douglas read the Greek myth of Euridice who is kept prisoner in the underworld for the winter and then allowed to return to the earth. Her mother is so happy to see her once more that she sings for joy and everything comes back to life. And the boy thought of his own mother, and of how everything felt like winter because she was there no longer. But he didn't say that to anyone, not even his own dad when he came home in the afternoon.

One day his dad went out to the garage and stood beside Ghostwing who was asleep in Teddy's old basket. He stood there and watched the goose for a long time. Then he opened the back window in the garage, the little window with its ledge just behind the shelf where Ghostwing was. He didn't say anything to Douglas; he didn't know if the boy would notice.

In the fields the geese were restless. They flew in their wide skeins each morning and evening as if they were practising, getting their wings ready for the long flight north to Iceland. Douglas' father watched them and listened to them, but he didn't say anything about them either to his son. He didn't know what to say and he didn't know what he hoped for either. He wanted to be a good father and to make Douglas happy, but there were some things he couldn't do. He felt that somehow he had failed, but he wasn't even quite sure how.

Douglas still talked to his goose. In the evening before he began his homework he went out and talked to Ghostwing. He told his goose everything, about the bullies in school and about being afraid. He spoke as Ghostwing snuffled about in the basket for lost bits of food. Sometimes his dad heard him, though he never came close to listen to what he was saying. But he heard the soft murmur of his voice in the shadows as he stood on the gravel in the drive.

*

It was the afternoon of school assembly. The hall was loud with children talking and shouting because Mrs Anderson hadn't arrived yet. Douglas' ears hurt with the noise; he wanted it to be over. It was supposed to be art this afternoon; he looked out of the windows of the hall and imagined he was drawing. He could feel the pencil in his hand.

'Hey, wakey wakey, Johnson!'

He was tugged from his dreamland by the shrieking of Alan Reardon behind him. The other boys roared with laughter and Alan Reardon tried to grab his arm. Douglas shrank away where he sat at the end of the bench. He wanted this to be over. He wanted to go back to the art room, to the quiet and the chance to draw.

Mrs Anderson came in at last, clapping her hands as she walked, and the quiet descended at once. Douglas' heart slowed; at least it would be better now she was here. At least the bullies couldn't get him.

'Now, those of you who're involved with swimming practice can leave at half past – just slip quietly out. But sadly I have to begin by mentioning the window that was broken at some point over the weekend – I want the culprit to own up before the week is up. I'm afraid it was someone from the school, so please have the courage and the honesty to come to my office and tell me.

'Now, a big well done to all of you who were involved with the chess championship. But the main reason for calling today's assembly is because I have just heard the results of the art competition for all the primary schools in the county. One or two of you will be hearing about your runners-up prizes, but I want you to know that the overall winner is Douglas Johnson. He'll be awarded his prize later on in the year, but I want to congratulate him today! This is a huge honour for him and for the whole school!'

They were clapping around him, everyone. A teacher was pushing him to his feet; he was to go out to the front. He felt as if he was swimming; everything was strange and far away. And then he saw the face of Abigail Edwards; her mouth was open as she looked at him, as she clapped too. Her face was full of astonishment, complete amazement. He saw the faces of all the bullies as he passed and went to the front, as the whole hall clapped and he shook Mrs Anderson's hand. It felt as though everything had gone into slow motion; the only thing he could hear was the sound of his own heart.

*

He ran all the way home. He ran so fast he was in danger of falling. The bullies watched him, said nothing as he flew past. He was different now; he had won the competition. But he had to get home. He vaguely saw the grey lines in the sky as he ran up the hill from the village, but he didn't think what they were – he didn't hear their voices and realise they were geese. He thought his heart would burst as he ran the last of the road and charged into the drive, his feet loud and careless on the gravel. His face was on fire and he was gasping for breath.

He stopped for a second then tore on down the drive, towards the garage and the ledge, the basket and his goose – Ghostwing. He wanted his goose to know, to know he had done it after all!

'Douglas! Douglas!'

He didn't hear his dad at first. He came in to the half-dark of the garage and stood there, dragging the air into his lungs as he searched for Ghostwing. Then he saw the shadow of his dad behind him.

'Douglas, he's gone! Ghostwing's gone!'

He looked at his dad and blinked and didn't understand. Then his dad was beside him, holding his shoulders.

'Your goose has gone, flown! He's gone back; he's on his way to Iceland!'

He looked at his dad in misery and disbelief. He turned away and couldn't believe his words. Not now, surely not now? His eyes blurred with tears and he broke away from his dad's hold. He heard him calling his name behind him, begging him to come back, but he couldn't. He had wanted his goose to know.

He dropped his bag on the gravel, went out onto the road, turned and saw the shadow of the wood. That was the only place he wanted to go. The wood where he'd always dreamed he'd see his mother, find her at last. He couldn't hear his dad behind him now. He could only hear his own feet and the thud of his heart in his chest. It was raining and it would be dark soon, but he didn't care – it didn't matter.

Ghostwing was gone and he hadn't even said goodbye.

*

This was where he had dreamed he would find his mum, in the heart of the wood. He remembered his dream, when she was there with him and he talked to her, and suddenly he saw her wings and she had gone, had flown away. But now it was Ghostwing that had flown away, before he had had a chance to say goodbye. He stood there in the half darkness, hearing the drops of rain pattering against the leaves, and he knew he would never find her there. Suddenly he knew that his dream was no more than fantasy, and he bent his head and cried because he did not know what to do. And his goose was gone.

'Dou-glas!'

He heard his dad calling his name a long way off. He didn't want to answer; he didn't want to explain any more. But his dad was worried; he could hear the anxiety in his voice as he called again and again. He didn't want to answer; he didn't want anyone to know where he was. He wanted to be on his own. But in the end he called back; he opened his dry mouth and answered.

When his dad found him he hugged him. And suddenly he realised his dad was crying too; his shoulders were shaking. When he let him go Douglas saw that his face was shining, and he knew it wasn't rain.

76

'Why are you crying, dad?' he asked. He remembered that the last time he had seen him crying had been at the hospital, the night his mum lay dying and there was nothing more they could do for her.

But now his dad smiled through his tears.

'I'm crying because I love you,' he said. 'That's the main reason. I'm crying because I'm worried for you, because I want you to be happy.'

'I won the art competition,' Douglas told him. 'I was coming home to tell Ghostwing; I wanted Ghostwing to know! Now it's too late!'

He cried again and this time his dad bent down beside him.

'No, Douglas, that's where you're wrong. Look what I found!'

His dad brought up his hand and it was the red notebook, the one he had found in his mum's room, in the house where she had once grown up. His dad opened it at the very back of the book and held it under the bough of a tree so no drops of water could reach it. And Douglas bent down and read.

I went out early today because the geese were coming back from Iceland. They were flying over the house to go down to the valley, to the fields where they always spend the winter. And I knew for the first time my father wouldn't shoot them; he has promised never to shoot another goose. I went out to watch them and it was a beautiful morning. I went out to the back of the house and I was watching the sky – the geese were only twenty feet above my head.

And then suddenly I saw a goose in front of me, just a few feet away. It had a tiny white mark on its forehead, just like Littlewing. And all at once I realised that it was Littlewing, that he had remembered and come back. As though to tell me everything was all right. I knelt down and called his name, but he didn't come any closer – he just looked at me. And I knew without a shadow of doubt it WAS Littlewing, that it could only be him!

Douglas finished and looked up. That was the end of the book, the very last page. Maybe that was why the notebook had been left there. His dad knelt beside him in the muddy, soaking ground.

'That's why you can't give up hope, Douglas! I believe your mum wanted you to find that, just as I believe she wanted you to draw Ghostwing! Look at all that's happened – I don't believe any of it has been an accident! And I really believe Ghostwing may come back, just like your mum's goose did. You have to believe, Douglas!'

He nodded. He looked at his dad's shining face and he nodded.

'Can we go back to the old house sometimes?' he asked softly. 'I feel mum there, somehow more than in the village. I love it up there.'

His dad nodded. 'I do too. Of course we can go back, maybe through the summer? How about that? We could even spend the holidays there.'

'And when the geese come back?' Douglas asked, his voice even softer.

'Yes,' his dad smiled. 'And when the geese come back.'

.

Author's dedication:

'This book is for Kate Scott, and for an old family friend, Ann Brown, a great bird lover.'

Kenneth Steven was the recipient of a Hawthornden Fellowship which enabled him to work on this novel in its entirety at Hawthornden Castle International Retreat for Writers in the winter of 2011. He would also like to thank all those who read the story and advised on its editing.

Kenneth Steven is best known as a poet but he's also a children's author. He's written many picture books (which are translated into some 14 languages) and novels for older readers. He works in primary schools across the UK and abroad, giving readings and leading writing workshops.

www.kennethsteven.co.uk

HAYWIRED
By Alex Keller

In the quiet village of Little Wainesford, Ludwig von Guggenstein is about to have his unusual existence turned inside out. When he and his father are blamed for a fatal accident during the harvest, a monstrous family secret is revealed. Soon Ludwig will begin to uncover diabolical plans that span countries and generations while ghoulish machines hunt him down. He must fight for survival, in a world gone haywire.

ISBN: 9781906132330
UK: £7.99

http://www.mogzilla.co.uk/haywired